Robbie's Robot

by Damian Harvey and Rory Walker

W
FRANKLIN WATTS
LONDON•SYDNEY

First published in 2015 by
Franklin Watts
338 Euston Road
London
NW1 3BH

Franklin Watts Australia
Level 17/207 Kent Street
Sydney
NSW 2000

FSC
www.fsc.org
MIX
Paper from
responsible sources
FSC® C104740

A CIP catalogue record for this book is available
from the British Library.

ISBN 978 1 4451 3950 0 (hbk)
ISBN 978 1 4451 3953 1 (pbk)
ISBN 978 1 4451 3952 4 (library ebook)
ISBN 978 1 4451 3951 7 (ebook)

Series Editor: Jackie Hamley
Series Advisor: Catherine Glavina
Series Designer: Peter Scoulding

Printed in China

Franklin Watts is a divison of
Hachette Children's Books,
an Hachette UK company.
www.hachette.co.uk

Robbie's room was
a tip, and Mum had
had enough!

"If you can't keep it tidy," she said, "there will be no pocket money for a month."

Robbie loved pocket
money. But he hated
tidying his room.
"It's too hard," he said.

6

"No it's not," said Mum. "Just see what's making it messy — and tidy it away."

Then Robbie had an idea.
He switched on his
computer and he
started to type.

"That's what I need," said Robbie. "A Clean-O-Matic Robot!"

Next morning there was a whoosh and a rumble, and something stopped outside.

"It's a parcel!" said Dad.

15

"Who is it for?" asked Mum.
"It's for me!" said Robbie.

Robbie's robot got to
work right away.

It tidied and polished.
It cleaned and it cleared.

Robbie's room
was spotless!

"Well done!" said Mum.

"It was nothing," said

Robbie.

The next day, Robbie's
room was as bad as ever.
"This is too hard," said
the robot.

"No it's not," said Robbie. "Just see what's making it messy – and tidy it away."

Robbie's robot looked at Robbie, then he looked out of the window...

"That's what I need,"
said the robot.

The next day, Robbie's room was spotless.

"It's perfect," said Mum.
"It was nothing," said
the robot.

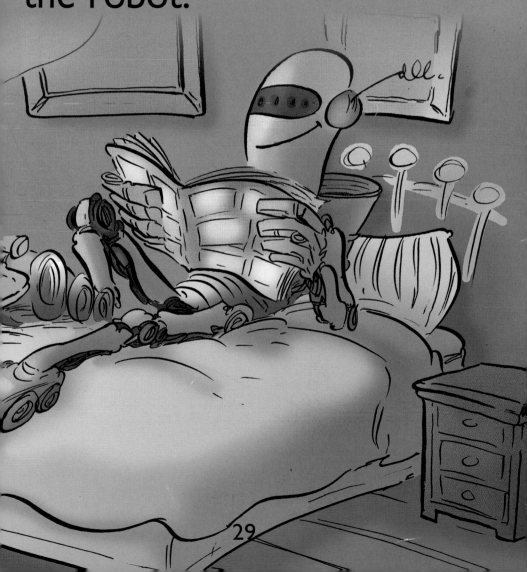

Puzzle 1

Put these pictures in the correct order.
Now tell the story in your own words.
How short can you make the story?

Puzzle 2

filthy   grubby

orderly

tidy   littered

spotless

Choose the words which best describe Robbie's room at the beginning and end of the story. Can you think of any more?

Answers

Puzzle 1

The correct order is:

1b, 2e, 3c, 4a, 5f, 6d

Puzzle 2

Room at the beginning: The correct words are filthy, grubby. The incorrect word is orderly.
Room at the end: The correct words are spotless, tidy. The incorrect word is littered.

Look out for more stories:

Mary and the Fairy
ISBN 978 0 7496 9142 4

The Bossy Cockerel
ISBN 978 0 7496 9141 7

Tim's Tent
ISBN 978 0 7496 7801 2

Sticky Vickie
ISBN 978 0 7496 7986 6

Handyman Doug
ISBN 978 0 7496 7987 3

Billy and the Wizard
ISBN 978 0 7496 7985 9

Sam's Spots
ISBN 978 0 7496 7984 2

Bill's Scary Backpack
ISBN 978 0 7496 9468 5

Bill's Silly Hat
ISBN 978 1 4451 1617 4

Little Joe's Boat Race
ISBN 978 0 7496 9467 8

Little Joe's Horse Race
ISBN 978 1 4451 1619 8

Felix and the Kitten
ISBN 978 0 7496 7988 0

Felix, Puss in Boots
ISBN 978 1 4451 1621 1

Cheeky Monkey's Big Race
ISBN 978 1 4451 1618 1

The Naughty Puppy
ISBN 978 0 7496 9145 5

Prickly Ballroom
ISBN 978 0 7496 9475 3

The Animals' Football Cup
ISBN 978 0 7496 9477 7

The Animals' Football Camp
ISBN 978 1 4451 1616 7

That Noise!
ISBN 978 0 7496 9479 1

The Wrong House
ISBN 978 0 7496 9480 7

The Frog Prince and the Kitten
ISBN 978 1 4451 1620 4

For details of all our titles go to: www.franklinwatts.co.uk